Choose your own dream

Julia Morris

Julia Morris

DEDICATION

For my children, Lottie and Freddie, thank you for dreaming your dreams with me.

Julia Morris

Contents

Introduction to Parents 1

How this Book Works.................................3

Relaxation 4

    Relaxation 1 - Breathing 4

    Relaxation 2 – Sense of Touch....................5

    Relaxation 3 Weightlessness.....................6

    Relaxation 4 – Counting 7

    Relaxation 5 – Body awareness 8

The Portals 9

Portal to Distant Places 9

The Field...10

    The Picnic 10

The Kite 13

    Cloud City..13

    Flying to the Stars 16

    Flying across the World 19

The Town...22

    The Market...23

    The Circus...26

    The Singing Garden 29

    The Starlight Cottage 32

The Forest..36

   The Fairy Village.................................36

   The Giant's Castle 40

The Talking Animals 43

   The Rabbit 43

   The Squirrel 46

   The Ladybug..49

The Beach..52

Under the Sea 53

   Mermaid City.......................................53

   The Dolphins 57

   The Pirate Hideout..............................60

   The Harbour..64

   The Jungle 64

The Arctic..68

   The Igloo 68

   Sledging with Elves 72

The Desert 75

   The Oasis...75

   The Caravan...79

The Mountains...82

   The Hot Air Balloon 82

The Dragon 86

The Unicorns..89

Portal to Distant Times 92

Jurassic Period 92

The Volcano...93

The Dinosaurs 96

Ancient Egypt 99

The Boat..99

The Temple 103

The Middle Ages 106

The Castle 106

The Knights..110

The Future...113

Techtopia 113

Ecopolis 118

Acknowledgement 122

The Mindmap...123

Choose your own dream

Introduction to Parents

Guided meditation is a practice that involves focusing the mind and relaxing the body through the use of visualisation and mindfulness. By practising breathing techniques and listening to a story, it leads to a calmer mind, and it can be used by people of all ages, including children. It is a safe and natural way to go to sleep that does not involve any medication or screen time. Young children often find it difficult to focus on breathing and meditation for longer periods, but by following a gentle story, they can keep their minds off their worries and softly drift off to sleep.

There are many benefits to practising guided meditation, including reduced stress, improved sleep, increased focus and concentration, and enhance overall well-being. It is a simple, yet powerful tool that can be incorporated into anyone's daily routine.

This book is a unique combination of a "choose your own adventure" story and guided meditation. It includes prompts for the reader to focus on their breath and imagine peaceful scenes similar to traditional guided meditation practices. However, instead of simply following a pre-determined path, the reader or the listener is given the opportunity to make choices and shape the direction of the journey, so the story will end differently each time, but always in a calming location to fall asleep in.

These stories are designed to inspire your child's imagination. Each chapter ends with a few questions that your child could focus on while going to sleep instead of fretting about the monster under their bed. Each chapter also includes a story idea that could be used the next day to encourage your child to draw a picture or to write or narrate their own story set in the beautiful locations that they have encountered.

We hope that you and your children can enjoy these stories together and that they will help you to fall asleep peacefully.

How this Book Works

This book can be read alone or out loud to another person listening. Before you start:

1.   Find a quiet, comfortable place to sit or lie down. It's important to have a space where you can relax and not be disturbed.

2.   Get comfortable. Wear loose, soft clothing and make sure you are in a comfortable position. You can sit in a chair with your feet planted on the ground, or you can lie down on a mat or bed.

3.   You can close your eyes or keep them open, whichever feels most comfortable for you. You can also place your hands on your lap or belly, or you can rest them on your knees.

4. Now read one of the five available relaxations. All of them are written to calm your breathing and prepare your mind to be open to the story, but in slightly different ways, so you can experience different ways of relaxation and after a while, you might have a favourite one.

5. Start the story with the description of the magical portals. At certain points, you will be asked to make a decision about what direction you want to go to. Make your choice and carry on reading on the given page number or follow the link on an eReader. The table of content at the beginning of the mindmap at the end of the book will help you find the right place if you want

to change your choice or skip parts when you read the book the next time.

6. The questions at the end of each storyline do not need to be answered straight away but could be something to think about while falling asleep and your ideas could be shared the next day. Feel free to leave them out if they get the mind too active.

Relaxation

Before we begin our journey, we need to relax our mind and body to be ready for the way ahead of us. Would you like to focus on your breathing (continue below), your sense of touch (page 05), feeling weightless (page 06), counting (page 07) or on your body (page 08)?

Relaxation 1 - Breathing

Welcome, to your dreamland. Before we start, we will focus on a very important and helpful skill: breathing. When we breathe deeply and slowly, it can help us feel calm and relaxed. It can also help us feel more focused and present in the moment.

So, let's take a few deep breaths together. Close your eyes, and take a deep breath in through your nose, filling your lungs with air. Hold it for a moment, and then slowly release the breath through your mouth, letting all of the air out. And again, take a deep breath in through your nose, hold it for a moment, and then slowly breathe out through your mouth.

As you focus on your breath and the peaceful place in your mind, let any worries or stress that you may be feeling just drift away. Imagine them being carried away by the breeze or melting away like snow. Take three more deep breaths, in through your nose, out of your mouth, two more, in and out and one more big one in and slowly out. Allow yourself to sink deeper into relaxation. When you're ready, we will begin our journey. Remember to keep focusing on your breath, and let it guide you into a peaceful, calming state of mind. (page 09)

Relaxation 2 – Sense of Touch

Welcome to your journey. Today, we are going to be focusing on our sense of touch. Touch is an important sense that helps us understand and interact with the world around us.

So, let's start by taking a moment to focus on the feeling of your bed. Close your eyes, and take a deep breath in. As you breathe out, allow yourself to sink deeper into your bed, feeling its softness and comfort. Notice the texture of your sheets and the way they feel against your skin. Notice the way your pillow carries your head and the way your blanket wraps you in warmth and cosiness. As you focus on the feeling of your bed, allow yourself to sink deeper into relaxation.

Let any worries or stress that you may be feeling just drift away – you know your bed is there, strong and safe and will carry you all through the night.

Take a few more deep breaths and let yourself fully sink into the feeling of your bed. When you're ready, we will begin our travels into other lands. (page 09)

Relaxation 3 Weightlessness

Before we travel to our dreamland, we need to free ourselves. Have you ever floated in the water and felt completely light as if you were floating on a cloud? That feeling of weightlessness can be very calming and relaxing.

So, let's take a moment to imagine ourselves floating weightlessly. Close your eyes, and take a deep breath in. As you breathe out, imagine yourself floating up into the air, away from the ground. As you float, imagine yourself becoming lighter and lighter, until you feel like you don't weigh anything at all. You are floating freely, like a feather on the breeze.

As you focus on the sensation of freedom, allow yourself to be more and more relaxed. Let any worries or stress that you may be feeling behind you while you float away. Imagine them being carried away by the wind or sliding down a rainbow.

Take a few more deep breaths and when you're ready, we will begin our story today. Remember to keep feeling light and relaxed, and let the story guide you into a happy sleep. (page 09)

Relaxation 4 – Counting

Welcome to your dreams. Start by finding a comfortable position and pay attention to your breath. Feel the rise and fall of your chest as you take a deep breath in through your nose and out through your mouth. With each breath, you are more and more relaxed.

Now, begin counting to 10. As you count, look at each number in your mind and notice how each number feels different. You might notice that some numbers feel lighter, and some feel heavier. Maybe the numbers even have different colours and textures. Think about each one as something new and with each number you feel more and more relaxed.

one, breathe in through your nose and out through your mouth,

two, breathe in and breathe out,

three, breathe,

four,

five,

six,

seven,

eight,

nine,

ten.

You are now more relaxed and calmer and are ready to go to a magical dreamland. (page 09)

Relaxation 5 – Body awareness

Before we go on a dream adventure, find a comfortable position, close your eyes and take a deep breath in through your nose and out through your mouth. As you breathe in, imagine a bright, white light filling up your heart. Feel the light spreading through your chest, filling your lungs and warming your back. As you continue to breathe deeply, imagine the light spreading to every part of your body. See it flowing through your shoulders, to your upper arms, then your lower arms and into every finger. You can feel your fingertips tingling with a nice sensation. Then it moves through your belly, down to your legs, filling the top of your legs, then your knees, down to the bottom of your legs. Your feet and toes are filled with warm, white light.

As you continue to breathe deeply, imagine the light becoming brighter and brighter, filling you with a sense of warmth and love. Allow yourself to fully relax and sink into the story. (continue below)

The Portals

You find yourself in your warm bed surrounded by your favourite toys. You are feeling calm and relaxed, and you are ready to begin your journey.

You suddenly notice something strange happening. A faint, glowing light begins to appear in your room, and it grows brighter and brighter, swirling and sparkling. Two portals appear in the corners of your room, one yellow and one green. You can't quite see what lies beyond them, but you know that the yellow one will lead you to places of magic and mystery and the green one to distant time periods.

Which of them is calling you today, the distant places (continue below) or the distant times (page 92)?

Portal to Distant Places

You take a deep breath, and then you step forward through the portal and you know that you are about to embark on a magical journey. On the other side, you find yourself on a crossroad, surrounded by rolling green hills and a clear blue sky.

You look around and see that there are three paths ahead of you. One path leads straight ahead, winding through the fields to a town (continue below). The second path leads into a green forest on the left (page 36), and a third path leads off to the right, where you can see the shimmering blue of the sea in the distance (page 52).

9

Which of the paths looks the most inviting?

The Field

You have decided to take the path through the fields and hills, and you begin to walk down the winding path. You enjoy the beauty of your surroundings but soon you start to notice that things are not quite as they seem. The flowers start to shimmer and sparkle as if they are made of diamonds. You realise that the birds are fantastical creatures, with rainbow-coloured wings and sparkling eyes, some with four wings, some with six. You continue down the path, and you see that it leads towards a small town in the distance. You can also see the sunshine on the field, which looks inviting and warm. Beyond the field, there is a kite waiting to take you up high.

Do you want to continue walking to the town (page 22), have a picnic in the field (continue below) or explore the sky with the kite (page 13)?

The Picnic

As you slowly walk across the field, you can feel the warm sunshine on your face. The grass is soft and springy under your feet, and you can hear the sound of birds singing in the distance. As you look around, you notice that the flowers in the field are not like any you've ever seen before. Each blossom is made entirely of sparkling crystals, and they seem to change shades as you look at them from different angles. The petals are thin and delicate, and they shimmer and sparkle in the sunlight, creating little rainbows on the grass below.

When you touch any of the blossoms, you feel a cool, smooth sensation against your skin, and they seem to fill you with good energy. Everywhere you can hear a faint, tinkling sound, like the sound of chimes that mixes with the chirping and singing of the birds.

When you reach the middle of the field, you come across a magical picnic blanket and basket. You can't wait to see what's inside, so you sit down and open the basket to find a feast of the most delicious and unusual foods you've ever seen. There are towering sandwiches, filled with layers of rainbow-coloured shimmering jam and others with nutty, melting cheese. There are bowls of sparkling fruit, each one a different shade of the rainbow. There are glasses of bubbly, sparkling drinks, filled with swirls of many colours.

You take a bite of a sandwich, and you are surprised by the burst of flavour that fills your mouth. It's sweet and tangy and spicy, all at the same time. You take a sip of the bubbly drink, and you feel the fizz tickling your tongue. You can't believe how delicious everything tastes. As you eat, you feel joy and contentment fill you up. You are so grateful for this magical picnic, and you know that you will always remember this experience.

You lie back on the soft, comfortable picnic blanket, surrounded by the glittering fields, and you start to drift off to sleep. The crystal flowers continue to create a soft melody with their tinkling sound as they sway in a light breeze above your head.

As you fall asleep, you think about the different colours of the birds and what they look like. You also think about the shapes and shades of the flowers and wonder what you would do with them if you could take some home. You hope that one day you will be able to understand the mystery of these crystal flowers.

Story idea: The flowers on the field were once ordinary daisies and poppies, how did they turn into crystals? And why did the king proclaim that no one is allowed to pick any flowers from this field?

The Kite

You walk across the field, and you see a beautiful kite in front of you, bright and colourful. You walk up to it and take hold of the string and straight away, the kite starts to rise into the sky. You look up and see that it is taking you on a special journey to a place high above. You can direct it to go to explore a city in the clouds (continue below), you could ask it to keep flying up and up to the stars (page 16) or you can continue flying the kite far across the world (page 19).

Cloud City

You direct your kite to fly higher and higher into the sky, and you start to see fluffy white clouds all around you. The sun is shining down on them, making the clouds look like they're made of pinkish gold. You're getting closer and closer to Cloud City, and you can see that it's a magical place made entirely out of clouds in lots of different shapes.

As you reach the city, you can see that there are clouds that look like houses and buildings, some look like gardens and parks, and others look like different animals. You gently land and take a walk to explore the city.

You come across a beautiful garden filled with all kinds of flowers made of clouds. They smell as sweet as candy and seem to gently glow from the inside. You find a playground where the swings, slides, and seesaws are also made of clouds, and when you come across a big trampoline made of clouds, it looks so fluffy and inviting that you can't resist the urge to jump on it. You take a running start and jump as high as you can. You feel like you're flying! You can see all of Cloud City from up here and it looks even more beautiful than before. You make big jumps and small jumps, somersaults, and handstands, trying lots of different moves and you are having so much fun.

When you start to get tired of bouncy, you continue to explore the city and come across other buildings made of clouds, such as a grand palace, a theatre, and even a library. The palace is made of the most elegant and intricate clouds, with tall spires and grand arches, while the theatre is made of fluffy clouds that look like they're ready to burst with laughter and music. The library is built of clouds that look like they can hold all the knowledge and stories in the world.

Soon the sky changes colour. The white clouds turn more and more pink, then purple, then blue, it is a beautiful sunset in the sky. You take a moment to enjoy the view and feel grateful for this amazing adventure. Night has fallen and you find a little house with a beautiful bedroom made entirely of clouds. The walls, the floor, and even the bed are made of the softest, fluffiest clouds you've ever seen. You walk inside and lay down on the bed. As you close your eyes, you can feel the clouds gently hugging you, making you feel safe and comfortable.

As you nod off, you think about the different rooms in the cloud house, what games you could play on the cloud playground, and what other buildings are there in Cloud City. You know that this is just the beginning of your adventure in Cloud City, and you can't wait to explore more of this magical place tomorrow.

Story idea: What happens when a group of young dragons discovers cloud city and moves it? How do they manage to rescue it from a raging storm sent by an evil magician?

Flying to the Stars

You suddenly notice that the kite is decorated with stars and planets, so you decide to ask it to fly higher up, all the way into space to explore the stars. You are amazed at how fast the kite is going, passing by the moon, planets, and asteroids. You can see different galaxies and nebulae, colourful and vibrant. Even though you are small compared to these giant planets, you feel part of something big and magical.

You fly by a shooting star and make a wish and you also come across a cluster of stars that form a beautiful shape that reminds you of a butterfly. As you continue your journey on the kite, you start to notice a planet in the distance. It looks like a beautiful blue and green marble. The kite starts to gently lower you down towards the surface of the planet and as you land, you notice that you feel a lot lighter than you did on earth. The planet has less gravity, so you feel like you're floating. You take a few steps and find that it's easy to jump and do a somersault in the air. It is so exciting to see how far and high you can jump. You start to imagine all the different games you could play on this planet, and how quickly you can get to places.

When you are all tired out, you notice that there is a cave opening on the side of one of the planet's mountains. You decide to investigate and bounce closer. You walk inside, you find that the cave is lit by a soft, blue light, that swirls on the cave ceiling and reflects from all walls which are made of smooth, grey rock. When you explore deeper into the mountain, you come across a beautiful underground moon pool, clear and deep. The water is shining with a light coming from below, shimmering in blue, turquoise and purple. Strange and beautiful fish swim in the pool, their scales reflecting the light in an otherworldly way.

You continue to walk around, and you feel your eyelids getting heavier and heavier. As you look for a place to rest, you notice a small alcove in the cave wall, and you lie down in a smooth hollow that feels like a comfortable hammock. The light from the glowing pool plays on the ceiling above you and the gentle noise of the underground stream lulls you to sleep.

As you watch the light and drift off, you think about the different planets you saw on your journey here and all their fascinating colours. You also wonder what strange and beautiful creatures live on this planet, and what kind of adventures you could have if you were to stay longer.

Story idea: This planet is inhabited by friendly aliens. What happens when a group of astronauts from earth land on this planet? And what adventures does one of the alien children get into when it hides in the astronauts' rocket and comes back to earth with them?

Flying across the World

You decide to explore the world with your kite, and you glide on and on, over mountains, forests, and oceans below you. After some hours, night-time falls over the world and your kite takes you over a beautiful fairy tale town. The houses are made of sturdy wood and brick, and they are decorated with colourful patterns and carvings. The streets are lit by torches that give off a warm and inviting light. You can see people walking around, some of them are dressed in amazing clothes, and you can hear the sound of music and laughter coming from the town square.

As you fly lower and take a closer look, you see a group of children playing a game of hide and seek in the square, laughing and having fun. Their parents are watching a group of musicians playing traditional music on the stage, lit by colourful lanterns, and many people are dancing and clapping along. You see a food market where vendors are selling treats like candy apples, warm pretzels and gingerbread cookies, and the delicious smells drift up to you in the air. The town is alive with activity and festivity, and you can't help but feel their enjoyment as you fly over it.

As you pass the town, you see a castle in the distance with a big drawbridge over a moat. You fly closer and you see that it's the home of the prince and princess who are looking out of the window, enjoying the view of the night and the town, just like you. They notice you and wave to you to invite you over. The prince and princess greet you warmly as you land on the castle's balcony. They are delighted to have you as their guest and take you on a tour of the castle. It is a grand and majestic palace, filled with beautiful paintings, tapestries, and sculptures. They show you the imposing banquet hall, the library filled with ancient books, and the throne room where the royal family holds court. The gardens are also a sight to behold, with flowers blooming all year round. They even show you the stables where the beautiful royal horses are kept and the castle's armoury where the guards keep their weapons. You can't help but feel a sense of awe as you walk through the castle.

Finally, they take you to your bed chamber for the night. The room is grand and has a four-poster bed with fluffy pillows and blankets. The room has a balcony that overlooks the town and the forest, the view is enchanting and serene. You can see the stars shining through the window, making you feel like you're still flying among them. The prince and princess bid you goodnight and you lay down on the bed and feel the soft mattress and the warm blankets. You close your eyes and let yourself sink into sleep, feeling safe and comfortable in this royal castle.

You think of all the things you saw on your flight

with the kite. You think back to the feeling of freedom as you were gliding over different landscapes and you remember the buildings and people you saw in the town. Just before you fall asleep you realise with a smile that you can come back and visit the fairy tale town and stay in the castle anytime you want.

Story idea: How did a poor shepherd use the magic kite to escape when he is falsely accused of stealing some bread? What exotic locations does the wind blow him to and how does he make his fortune?

The Town

As you continue down the path, the rolling green fields give way to a magical little town. Some houses are tall and slender, with pointed roofs and sparkling windows. Some are square and small, made of shimmering stones or smooth polished wood, while others are built on stilts or shaped like giant mushrooms. Brightly coloured glass and roofs that shimmer like stars catch your eye. You can't wait to explore the secrets and stories this town holds.

As you enter, strange and fantastical creatures walk in the streets. Tall elves with pointed ears and sparkling eyes, short goblins with sharp teeth, winged and scaled creatures, and those with fur and hooves, all bustling about. You come to a crossing: Straight ahead you see a busy market, filled with strange and unusual goods. The left leads to a circus with bright colourful tents and to the right you see a special garden filled with rare and exotic plants and strange noises. Further on, you also notice a particularly sparkling house in the distance. Do you visit the market (continue below), the circus (page 26), the special garden (page 29) or will you knock on the door of the sparkling house (page 32)? Take a moment to choose where your curiosity leads you.

The Market

As you walk through the market, you soon realise it is a fair for wizards. You see all sorts of strange and magical sights and sounds. There are stalls selling potions and spells, and people haggling over the price of rare and unusual ingredients. The colourful stalls sell all sorts of strange objects, from glowing crystals to talking animals, glowing, shimmering lanterns, bags of glittering fairy dust and magic wands.

You explore the market and come across a stall that catches your eye. It's filled with all sorts of magical pets, from talking birds to tiny dragons that breathe fire. You see a small, fluffy creature that looks like a cross between a cat and a fox, with soft, fluffy blue fur. It looks up at you with big, bright eyes and your heart is filled with love. The vendor tells you that it's a "Familiar," a magical pet that can help you with your spells and potions, and that it is called Whisp. You can't resist its charm and decide to buy it. The vendor gives you a small bag filled with food and instructions on how to take care of it. Whisp rubs against your chest and purrs as you pet it, and you can't help but feel a sense of joy and excitement at the thought of having such a magical companion. You hold Whisp close to you and continue to explore the market, feeling grateful that you have found a new friend.

You continue to wander around, and as you see a

table with potion ingredients that bubble and fizz, you can't resist the temptation to buy a few items. You haggle with the vendors to get the best prices and look forward to trying out your new items. Amongst the potions on the market table, you notice one labelled "Sleeping Elixir," and you really want to try it. You buy it for a good price and take a sip. Almost immediately, you feel sleepiness wash over you. You feel your body relax and your mind quiet, and you lie down in a nearby hammock and start to sink into a peaceful sleep, with Whisp curled up at your side. You feel safe and protected, surrounded by the magic, and wonder of the wizards' market.

As you drift off, you start to think about the different potions you saw at the market. You remember the colours, shapes, and smells of each potion, and wonder about the magical powers they could give you. You imagine choosing one of the wands and wonder what it would look like. As you sleep, you dream of strange and magical places, filled with talking animals and flying wizards. You feel a sense of peace and contentment, knowing that you are safe and protected in this magical world.

Story idea: What happened when you bought a potion and tried it out without knowing what it will do? And why did Whisp have to help you escape from the purple wizard?

Choose your own dream

The Circus

As you walk towards the circus, you hear the sound of laughter and music filling the air. You hear trumpets and drums, and people cheering and clapping. The air is filled with the scent of popcorn and cotton candy, and there is a smell of animals and sawdust. This circus is a place of wonder and imagination, where anything is possible.

You sit in the front row in the tall round tent, mesmerised by the sights and sounds of the circus. You can feel the energy and excitement in the air, and you can't believe the things you are seeing. There are people dressed in all sorts of fantastical costumes, acrobats who seem to defy gravity and juggle fire at the same time and tightrope walkers who balance on a thin wire high in the sky. You see animals that you have never seen before, from talking lions to flying unicorns, gryphons, and dragons. All of them are performing tricks that seem impossible.

At last, Madame Mystique, the star of the show, comes into the tent. She is a tall, slender magician with long, flowing hair and sparkling eyes. She is dressed in a shimmering, sequined suit that catches the light in a way that makes her look almost like a star-filled sky.

She stands in the centre of the circus ring, holding a wand in her hand. She waves the wand in the air, and a shower of sparks and glitter fills the air. The magician makes an elephant disappear and brings a giant dragon in its place, making the audience go wild with excitement. Next, she reaches into her hat and pulls out a small creature with rainbow-coloured wings and white, fluffy fur that seems to shoot sparkles in all directions. The audience cheers and claps as the magical creature flutters its wings and takes off into the air, in a shower of colourful sparks. Everyone is hypnotised by her tricks, and they can't help but be amazed as they watch her perform. She is a true master of her craft.

As the circus show comes to an end, you are full of joy and contentment. You know that you will always remember your visit to this place, and you can't wait to come back and see more. But you've been walking and exploring for hours, and you can't help but feel a little bit tired.

You see a row of colourful circus caravans in the distance, and you decide to take a closer look. You see wagons painted in all sorts of bright, vibrant colours. You wonder what it would be like to live in one of them, travelling from place to place, performing in front of different audiences every night.

You decide to take a rest here, and you find a cosy little bed in the corner of one of the caravans. As you drift off, you think about the show you just watched. You try to remember all the tricks the magician performed, what the acrobats looked like, and what animals live in the circus. You imagine yourself performing exciting stunts and being a part of this magical world.

Story idea: How did the lion learn to talk? And how did it come about that he is best friends with the unicorn, and they are travelling with the circus now?

The Singing Garden

As you walk through the town, you see a garden in the distance with bright, colourful flowers that seem to be singing and dancing in the breeze. You feel curious to find out more and eager to see the enchanted plants up close. As you approach the garden, you can smell the sweet fragrance of the flowers and hear the soft melody of their songs.

You enter the garden and see that the flowers are even more beautiful and magical than you could have imagined. You see flowers with petals that shimmer and sparkle like diamonds, and some with blossoms that glow with a soft, warm light. Some flowers change colour and pattern every time the wind touches them and there are some with petals that are made of soft, fluffy clouds. There are flowers that are little honey fountains, with the sweet nectar cascading down from their centre like a waterfall. You admire the flowers with petals that look like they're made of delicate, iridescent feathers, and the ones with petals that resemble a starry night sky, and you are careful not to step on the flowers with petals that resemble beautiful, intricate stained-glass windows.

Each of these flowers is unique and possesses its own enchanting qualities, from the way they move in the breeze to the way they catch the light, but the most beautiful are the flowers with petals that seem to dance and sing. The singing flowers are the tallest plants you can see here, with petals in patterns that you have never seen before. You hear a soft, gentle hum that seems to fill the air, and you hear a faint, tinkling sound that seems to come from the grass. All the flowers' leaves gently move in time to the music, and you can't stop your feet from tapping along as well.

As you look around the garden, you notice tiny specks darting and twirling in the air. These are the insects, doing an aerial dance to the music of the singing flowers. The insects in the garden are truly unique creatures with delicate wings that shimmer in the sunlight in colours that range from iridescent greens and purples to bright pinks and yellows. They come in all shapes and sizes, some have long, slender bodies while others are plump and round. They are graceful flyers, making smooth turns and spirals in the air. They fly and spin, their movements graceful and effortless, as if they are part of a choreographed performance. Their wings beat quickly, creating a soft rustling sound that blends with the music of the singing flowers. They fly in perfect harmony, as if they have rehearsed their dance for years. You can see the joy in their movements, as they twirl and loop, chasing each other in an endless dance. All of them seem to be celebrating life, and the beauty of nature and the magic of this special place.

You sit a while, watching the insect dance, but then your eyes are starting to get heavy. You've been walking a long way to get to this garden, and you are starting to feel a little bit tired. You find a cosy little spot and lie down in the soft, dry grass, with the gentle song of the garden all around you. The flowers gently sing you to sleep, and you glide into dreams, knowing that you can always come back to this place.

As you fall asleep, you think about all the unusual flowers and insects in this garden. You try to remember which of the singing flowers is your favourite and what melody it sings. You imagine the different types of insects that buzz around the garden, and you wonder what the garden looks like from their perspective.

Story idea: What happens when a witch comes into the garden to brew a potion out of the singing flowers? What would the potion do? And who rescues the flowers?

The Starlight Cottage

Your eyes are drawn to small a cottage in the distance that seems to twinkle mysteriously. As you walk towards the cottage, you see that it glows with starlight. It is a small, charming structure with a round, shining roof that looks like a full moon and the walls of the cottage seem to be covered with shimmering, sparkling stars.

You feel excited as you come closer, and as you knock on the door, a magical little man opens it and looks at you with a warm and welcoming smile. The man is a small, wizened figure with twinkling eyes and a kind, gentle face. He is dressed in a long, flowing robe with moons and stars embroidered on it, and the robe seems to shimmer and sparkle with a magical light. It seems like the colour of the robe shifts and changes, glowing blue with all shades of the night sky.

The little man greets you and invites you in, and you can feel his kindness and compassion radiating from him. You step inside, and see the cottage is filled with all sorts of strange and magical objects and artefacts. You see shelves and cabinets filled with bottles and vials, and a workbench covered in many mysterious tools and instruments.

Of course, the little man must be a master of magic! You watch as he waves his wand and makes objects appear and disappear and turns a bottle into a rose. He seems very focused and determined as he works at his table on a new spell. This spell, if successful, will mean no one will ever have to do housework again. You feel a sense of respect for the wizard's magical abilities, and you are very hopeful that he will be successful in his quest for this spell.

He delves deep into his magic books, searching for the perfect incantation. He mumbles to himself, trying different combinations of words and gestures, determined to find the right one. You can see the concentration etched on his face as he experiments with different ingredients, mixing them together to create the perfect potion. With a flick of his wand, he sprinkles the potion on the spell book, and suddenly the pages start to glow with a warm light. The wizard's face lights up with excitement as he sees the spell starting to take shape. You can feel the magic in the air, and you hold your breath, waiting to see what will happen next.

He raises his wand, pointing it at the spell book, and utters the final incantation in a voice filled with confidence. With a loud pop, the mist forms into a shimmering ball of light that hovers in the air for a moment, spreading around the room and suddenly everything is clean and tidy!

The wizard lets out a triumphant laugh as he looks around the room, and you can see the happiness and pride in his eyes. He turns to you with a smile, and says, "My dear child, I have done it! The spell is complete, and you will never have to do tidying up again." You can feel the warmth of his happiness radiating from him, and you know that you have witnessed a true moment of magic.

Now that the excitement is over, you are ready for a nap. In the corner of the wizard's library, you spot a beautiful and comfortable wooden bed built into the wall, with the ceiling above covered in shining stars. You decide to have a little nap here and find that the bed is the softest and most comfortable bed you have ever slept in. You close your eyes and sink into a feeling of a sense of peace and contentment.

While you are resting in the starlight bed, you think about what magical items there are in the cottage, and you wonder what would happen if you drank one of the magical potions. You try to imagine what magic the wizard could do to help you on your way and what stories you could read in his magical library.

Story idea: How did the wizard save the town when it was attacked? Why is the wizard living in a house made out of starlight and not in the castle that the king gave him?

Choose your own dream

The Forest

You soon reach the mysterious, magical wood, and see that it is unlike any other wood you have ever been in. The forest is filled with trees that have all kinds of interesting shapes, forming animals and objects. In front of you is a tree shaped like a giant elephant, with a trunk and tusks made of branches. Next to it is a tree shaped like a big dragon, with wings made of leaves and flames made of red flowers. A little further on you spot a tree that looks like a giant robot, with gears and gadgets made of wood.

You keep wandering, admiring the strange trees until reach a clearing with different paths out of it. To one side of the clearing, you see some talking animals (page 42). The left path seems to lead to a fairy village (continue below) and the right path leads out of the forest to a giant's castle in the distance (page 40). Which way are you going to go?

The Fairy Village

You decide to visit the fairy village, you have always wondered how the fairies live. As you stroll around the tiny village, you seem to be getting smaller and smaller until you are the same size as the fairies around you. You admire their beautiful village with tiny tree houses that are not just small and delicate, but also intricately crafted and adorned with masterful details. Between the houses you see fairies with hair braided with flowers, and their clothes are sewn with glittering beads and sequins. You see them tending to their gardens, where they grow all sorts of strange and exotic plants, like flowers that change scent when they are touched, or plants that glow in the dark. You see them tending to their animals, which are tiny furry creatures some with stripey and some with spotted fur and many of them seem to have magical abilities.

As you walk through the fairy village, you see a beautiful and regal fairy queen sitting on her throne. She sees you and beckons you to come closer. The queen of the fairies has long, flowing hair that is the colour of gold with a hint of green. Her eyes are bright and dark green, and they seem to dance with magic and mischief. She wears a crown of diamonds and emeralds on her head and her wings are large and sparkle in the sunlight that falls through the forest canopy. She is wise and knowledgeable, and she is always happy to share her wisdom with those who seek it, so she teaches you the importance of looking after the forest and preserving its natural beauty and resources. She emphasizes the importance of taking care of the trees, plants, and wildlife that make the forest their home, and how all living things are interconnected and dependent on one another. She also encourages you to be mindful of your own actions and explains how they impact the environment, reminding you to be respectful and leave no trace when exploring the forest. Through her teachings, the queen instils a love and appreciation for nature in you, encouraging you to be a protector and guardian of the forest for future generations.

After her lesson, she takes you by the hand and leads you to her tree house, which is nestled high up in the branches of a giant tree. The fairy house is a truly magical place. Everything inside the house is made from things you can find in the forest, and everything is imbued with magic and wonder. You see a table made of twigs and leaves, with a chair made of acorns and there is a shelf filled with books made of leaves and bark, with pages made of petals. In the corner, there is a bed carved out of a pinecone, with a mattress of soft moss and ferns and a blanket made of delicate flowers. As you see the bed, you realise how tired you are, and you feel a sense of peace and happiness as you lie down in it. You close your eyes and fall asleep, dreaming of flying with the fairies.

While you are falling asleep, you try to imagine what the furry animals are called and what the cutest ones look like. You think about what you would put into your own fairy treehouse and how you could use the things you find in the woods. What would it be like to fly with fairy wings and what stories will the fairy queen tell you tomorrow?

Story idea: The fairy queen was once a normal girl, how did she become the ruler of the fairies? And what skills did she use to save the fairies from the naughty gnomes?

The Giant's Castle

You decide to take the path to the giant's castle, and it is much closer than you thought because it is so large. The castle is a huge and imposing structure, made of stone and wood. It towers above the trees, built on a giant rock, and it seems to stretch up towards, all the way to the sky. You knock on the giant's door, and to your surprise, the giant who opens it, is friendly and welcoming. He invites you inside and allows you to explore the castle and see all of the giant things that it has to offer.

The master of the castle leads you through his palace, filled with pride, and you see all sorts of strange things. In the kitchen, you see a giant stove and oven, with pots and pans hanging from the ceiling that are big enough for you to have a bath in. You see a giant shelf, filled with all kinds of strange and exotic foods that could feed a whole town for a week. The sink is bigger than a swimming pool, with a tap that is as tall as you are.

You come across the giant's bedroom, which has a giant bed with sheets and blankets as big as a football field. You see a giant wardrobe big as a house and a giant mirror that reflects your tiny figure next to the giant's. Next, you visit the giant's library. It's filled with huge books, with pages as big as posters.

Finally, the giant takes you to the castle's rooftop

garden. The garden is filled with giant flowers and plants, some as tall as the giant himself. You see massive butterflies and bees as big as dogs and just as playful. The garden is a peaceful and serene place, and you feel a sense of calm as you take in the sights and sounds around you.

As evening falls, you go downstairs to the living room, where you find a giant fireplace, with logs the size of tree trunks. You see a giant sofa and chairs, with pillows and cushions as big as your bed. Seeing these big soft pillows reminds you that you are very sleepy, and you decide to have a rest here. The giant lifts you onto a chair and you curl up on it like a cat. You know that you are safe from everything in here with the giant protecting the castle, and your eyes soon shut.

As you rest, you can think about all the other giant rooms in the castle and what you could find there. You think back to the kitchen: what would it be like to eat one of the giant's sweet treats? Then you remember the giant fluffy bees and smile as you imagine taking one home as a pet and think of all the fun games you could play together.

Story idea: How did the giant become friends with a tiny mouse? And why does the mouse wear a crown?

The Talking Animals

You are curious to find out more about the talking animals and you go over to them. You see a rabbit, a small, fluffy creature, with long ears and a stubby tail (continue below). Next to him sits a squirrel, beautiful and red with a bushy tail. It chatters at you, and you see that it is holding a small acorn in its paws (page 46). A shiny little ladybug flutters towards you and smiles at you (page 49). Who do you want to visit today?

The Rabbit

The rabbit wiggles its ears and hops off, and after a second of hesitation, you start following it. As you walk, you begin to shrink down until you are the same size as the rabbit.

You arrive at the entrance of the rabbit's burrow and are amazed by the complexity of the underground network of tunnels and chambers. The walls and ceilings are made of rich, dark earth, and the air is filled with the familiar smell of home. You follow the rabbit through the winding tunnels, and with each step, you discover more and more of the burrow's hidden wonders. Each room you come to is spacious, round, and comfortable and filled with members of the rabbit family. The first room you go to is a storeroom, filled with rows and rows of delicious-looking berries and fresh, crisp carrots. The colours are vibrant, and the aromas are tantalising, making your mouth water. As you continue your exploration, you come across a playroom, where tiny, fluffy bunnies are hopping and playing together. They are so cute and full of energy, their tiny noses twitching with excitement. You just have to stay and play with them for a little bit, and they let you join in with their bunny games.

As you continue to explore the other rooms, you meet all sorts of other rabbits living in the burrow, each one with its own unique personality and appearance. Some are shy and reserved, while others are outgoing and playful. Each rabbit tells you their name, and you meet Daisy, Willow and Hazel, Coco and Bugs, Bunbun and Snowball and many others and they are all happy to stop and have a little chat with you.

Eventually, you come to a cosy sleeping den, where a nest of hay is made in the corner, with a soft and fluffy blanket made of grass and flowers. The hay smells good of summer on the field, and you feel your eyelids becoming heavy. As you curl up in the hay bed, some of the bunny babies come and snuggle up to you and keep you warm and cosy and you can feel their warm fur around you, as you glide into sleep.

As you are lying there, think about what other rooms in the rabbit burrow and what rabbits live there. What do look like and what are their names? You remember how you played with the baby bunnies and their fun games, what did you play together?

Story idea: What happens when one of the rabbit children decides to leave the burrow to go on an adventure? And how does the fairy queen help it to get home?

The Squirrel

As you follow the chatty squirrel, he introduces himself as Sam. You follow him through a lush, green forest. The sun is shining and the leaves rustle in the wind, filling the air with the sweet scent of nature. With surprise, you notice that you are getting smaller and smaller until you are the same size as Sam. He invites you to hold onto his back and you feel his soft fur, and you know he is a strong and skilled climber. Sam chatters away as he gracefully climbs the tree with you on his back, leaping from branch to branch with ease. Finally, you reach his home, a cosy nest high up in the tree. As you enter the hole, you see that it is filled with soft leaves and twigs, creating a warm and comfortable space. You see Sam's family all gathered around, chatting and playing. There is his mom, Sally, his dad, Simon, and his little sister, Sophie.

Sally is busy gathering acorns and nuts to store for the winter, carefully selecting the best ones to add to her collection. Simon is helping Sophie learn how to climb trees, guiding her as she tries her best to scamper up the trunk. Sophie is determined, but she keeps slipping and sliding back down. With a smile, you join in, and you and her family help Sophie reach the very top of the tree. From here, you can see the entire forest stretched out before you. The leaves of the trees dance in the breeze and the birds sing a joyful song. You feel happy being part of this little family as you all enjoy the beauty of nature together.

Soon the sun starts to set, casting a warm orange glow over the forest. You climb back down to the nest and Sally starts preparing a delicious dinner with the food that she had gathered earlier. She invites you to join them and you are very grateful to be able to stay a bit longer. Sam and Sophie are setting the table, laying out acorn bowls and pinecone cups while Simon is collecting water to drink.

As you all sit down to eat together, Sally serves you a delicious stew made of berries, nuts and vegetables. The flavours are amazing, and you find yourself enjoying the meal as you chat and laugh with the family. Sam tells you about his adventures in the forest, Sophie shows you her drawings of her favourite trees and Sally shares her recipe for her famous acorn bread. It's a cosy and warm meal, and as darkness falls, the family invites you to spend the night in the nest, and you say goodnight feeling happy and full.

In the corner of the nest, you see a nice little bed made out of soft leaves and moss and as you lie down, Sophie and Sam lie down next to you and cover you with their fluffy tails to keep you warm until you wake up again.

As you nod off, you think of the delicious food that mum Sally makes out of nuts and berries. You think about the fun games that Sam and Sophie like to play with the other animals that live in this tree, and you try to imagine what it would be like to learn to live in the forest with the animal children.

Story idea: How did Sophie one day overcome her fear of climbing to rescue her brother? And how did they work together to trick the mean old crow?

The Ladybug

You decide to make friends with the ladybug and introduce yourself. She tells you that her name is Lily and invites you to come along. You happily accept and follow Lily as she crawls across the leaves and the longer you follow Lily the Ladybug, the smaller you get until you are the same size as her. Soon you find yourself walking through a beautiful garden, the sun is shining, and the flowers are in full bloom, filling the air with their sweet fragrances. Walking alongside Lily, you notice that the world looks different from her perspective. The leaves tower above you like giant green umbrellas, and the flowers are enormous and colourful. You come across a small pond with lily pads floating on the surface. Lily tells you that this is her favourite spot in the garden, and she often comes here to take a nap in the sun. The pond is filled with all sorts of interesting creatures, from tadpoles to dragonflies. You also spot a family of frogs sitting on a nearby rock, croaking softly to each other. Lily leads you to a small waterfall and you listen to the soothing sound of the water as it cascades into the pond. The mist from the waterfall creates a rainbow and you feel like you've stepped into a fairy tale. Lily shows you how to catch water droplets on your tongue and you both giggle with delight.

You leave the pond and climb on a tall rose, which is

quite hard now that you are so tiny. You see all sorts of insects going about their business, among them a busy bee buzzing from flower to flower, gathering nectar. You watch as the bee flies over to a white flower and lands on the petals and you go over to have a chat with her. The bee looks at you with her big, friendly eyes and introduces herself as Bella. She asks if you would like to join her as she gathers nectar for her hive. You happily accept and ride on Bella's back as she flies from flower to flower. You see all sorts of beautiful flowers in the garden, not just roses and daisies, but strange and exotic flowers you've never seen before. You watch as Bella uses her long, sticky tongue to slurp up the sweet nectar from the flowers and she gives you a few drops of the sugary, delicious liquid.

As Bella drops you off next to Lily again, you find a small teacup, that's been left behind by a garden visitor, and you and Lily sit in it and enjoy the view and fragrant smell of tea that still lingers in the cup. Lily tells you all sorts of interesting stories about her life in the garden, and you know you are becoming good friends as you spend time together.

As the sun starts to set and the garden begins to change, Lily takes you under a hollow log, where you find a cosy little spot to rest on the moss. Before you fall asleep, you think you see a beautiful white moth with soft fur and big wings flutter past you, but you are very tired and know, you will have to come back another time to explore the garden at night.

As you lie here, you think about what insects live in the garden, and what it would like to spend every day as one of them. You remember the strange flowers that you have seen growing here, seeing their beautiful colours and shapes in your mind's eye. You wonder what magical creatures you could meet in the garden at night and with that, you let the peaceful tranquillity of the garden lull you into a deep and restful sleep.

Story idea: What happened when the beautiful moth fell in love with the vain butterfly? Why did the bee have to save the moth and the butterfly from danger?

The Beach

You head down the path towards the seaside and soon reach a beautiful beach lying in the sunshine. As you step onto the sand, you suddenly realise that the grains between your toes is not the usual dull, pale colour, but a gleaming, golden yellow and you realise it is pure gold dust that sparkles in the sunlight and feels soft and cool to the touch. You bend down and scoop up a handful of sand, letting it run through your fingers. As you do, you notice that the sand has a spicy smell - a blend of cinnamon, turmeric and ginger that reminds you of exotic places.

You walk along the shore, letting the waves wash over your feet and suddenly you notice something in the water, splashing about that seems to invite you in (continue below). Further along the beach is a harbourside, with a grand sailing ship, waiting to take you far away (page 64). And not far off the beach in the water you can spot a mysterious island (page 60). Which one would you like to explore further?

Under the Sea

The sea looks tempting, and you dive into the waves. You feel the cool water envelop you as you swim deeper and deeper, and you are surprised to find that you can breathe underwater. You see all sorts of colourful fish swimming alongside you - bright red, orange, and yellow fish, and shimmering silver fish with long, flowing tails.

As you swim, you see a distant glimmer in the distance, and you realise it is a mermaid city under the sea (continue below). On your other side, you see a pod of dolphins swimming nearby who seem to invite you to play with them (page 57). Where would you like to swim to today?

Mermaid City

The sun is shining through the ocean surface, painting golden streaks in the water and inviting you to explore the depths below. You decide to see the underwater city closer up and as you swim through this marine world, you see all sorts of fascinating sights - houses made of shells and coral, gardens filled with colourful seaweeds, and streets lined with gleaming pearls. The houses are decorated with swirling details, each one a unique and beautiful creation.

You see mermaids and mermen swimming about, going about their daily business. Some are busy tending to their gardens, filled with exotic and rare sea plants, while others are chatting with their neighbours, exchanging stories and gossip. You see a group of young mermaids and mermen playing a game amongst the coral reefs, playing fetch with small fish and their laughter rises up in bubbles.

As you continue to explore, you get closer and closer to the grand palace at the centre of the city. The palace is a magnificent structure, built of shimmering pearls and adorned with intricate carvings of sea creatures and plants. You see the merking sitting on his throne, surrounded by his advisors and attendants. He sees you and allows you to approach.

As you glide inside, you see that the king is a handsome merman with short, curly hair the colour of gold. He has a strong, confident face, and his eyes shine with intelligence. He is willing to share some of his stories about the rich history of the mermaid kingdom and bids you to sit on a rock near his throne. You discover that the kingdom was founded by a group of mermaids and mermen who were tired of living in the shadows of the human world. They decided to create a place where they could live freely and openly, celebrating their unique culture and way of life. They searched the ocean for the perfect location and eventually found a secluded bay, surrounded by lush coral reefs and teeming with sea life, but they had to fight great wars against sea monsters and rival underwater cities before they could build their beautiful city here. You listen in awe as he recounts the stories of how his ancestors faced these challenges, and how they were able to overcome them.

He also tells you about the different customs and celebrations of the merpeople. One of the most important traditions is the annual "Ocean's Bounty Festival". During this festival, the mermaids and mermen gather to give thanks for the abundance of fish, shellfish, and other sea creatures that provide them with food and livelihood. They also give thanks for the protection of the mergods that keep them safe from other dangers in the ocean.

The Bounty Festival is a grand and joyful event, with music, dancing, and feasting. The mermaids and mermen decorate the city with shells and seaweed and prepare a feast of delicious seafood dishes, such as grilled fish, crab cakes, and clam chowder and there are competitions and games, such as a race through the coral reef, and a treasure hunt for pearls and shells. The festival is a reminder of their reliance on the sea and the need to protect and preserve it for future generations. You listen to the king's stories with wonder and respect and feel very lucky to be able to find out more about the underwater world.

When the king sees that you are getting tired, he

invites you to stay in a room in his palace. The room is grand and luxurious, decorated with starfish and corals. In the centre of the room is a giant seashell bed, and you lie down in it. The inside of the shell is soft and comfortable, with a heap of fluffy blankets and pillows. You feel the gentle rocking of the waves as you glide into dreams.

As you drift off to sleep, you imagine all the creatures that live in this underwater city, ponder what the schools for the young mermaids and mermen is like and what kind of skills they learn there. You imagine yourself swimming and exploring this underwater world, meeting new creatures and discovering new things every day and gently drift off to sleep.

Story idea: The mermaid king was once a humble dolphin-herd, but he managed to save the mermaid princess. Why was she in danger and how did he save her?

The Dolphins

The dolphins seem to have a good time, and when you wave to them, they wave back with their fins and invite you to come and play. Excitedly, you quickly swim over and join in their fun. The dolphins are friendly and playful, and they seem to be enjoying themselves as much as you are.

You notice that the more you play with the friendly creatures, the more you can understand their communication and the more you feel at home in the water. You feel so much joy and energy as you swim alongside the dolphins, diving and flipping through the water and you are amazed at how fast and easy you can swim now. They teach you how to play different games like tag, hide and seek and how to mimic different sea creatures' moves and sounds.

After a while, the dolphins challenge you to a race. You accept and the race begins. You swim as fast as you can, with the dolphins swimming alongside you. You need all your determination and focus as you compete. Nearing the finish line, you put on a burst of speed and cross it first. The dolphins cheer and clap their flippers. You are filled with pride and happiness as you bask in the glow of your win. You think you can now understand what the dolphins are saying and you work out their names, so you know now that the one who initiated the race is called Flash, the one who taught you how to mimic sea creatures is called Echo, and the one who has been your guide throughout the race is called Breeze.

The race was fun, but now you are exhausted and ready to have a rest. The dolphins guide you to a cosy underwater cave. The cave is calm and safe, with soft, sandy floors and walls lined with shiny pearls. You cuddle up in the soft sand and listen to the sound of the dolphins singing outside. Their songs are different from any that you have ever heard before, with a harmonious melody that fills your heart with peace and contentment.

As you drift off, you think about the many adventures you have shared with your new dolphin friends. You imagine swimming with them in the open ocean, exploring shipwrecks and coral reefs, and discovering new sea creatures. You think about their favourite games and the different sea creatures they have introduced you to. You let the peaceful swaying of the ocean lull you into a deep and restful sleep, feeling grateful for the experience and looking forward to the next time you can come back to visit your new marine friends.

Story idea: One day, a dolphin boy fell in love with a seal girl. What adventures does he have to go through to win her heart?

The Pirate Hideout

As you stroll along, you find a small, wooden boat on the beach and row out to sea. The water is calm and clear, and you can see the sun glistening on the surface, creating a mesmerising dance of light and shadows. You can hear the seagulls overhead and see a small island on the horizon, its lush green foliage and sandy beaches beckoning you to come closer. You arrive at the shore, tie up the boat and step out onto the sand, and set out to explore the island, eager to discover all its secrets.

As you wander around the island, you come across a small, hidden cove with a secret hideout filled with friendly and welcoming pirates who don't mind you walking between the pirate huts, and exploring their small settlement, where you see all sorts of interesting sights - a kitchen with a pot of boiling stew, a pier where the pirates are mending their nets, and a workshop where they are working on fixing their swords.

As you explore the island, the pirates come up to you with a surprise. They have organised a treasure hunt just for you! They tell you that they have hidden a treasure somewhere on the island and it's your job to find it. They give you a map and a compass and set you off on your adventure.

You start you search for the X that marks the spot

and follow a hidden path until you come to a dense jungle. As you make your way through the thick foliage, you hear the sound of running water. You follow the sound and soon you come across a beautiful waterfall. You head straight through the refreshing water and behind it find a hidden exit that leads you to the base of a tall hill. You start to climb to the top, and suddenly find a strange hut with a sail sticking out of it as if it was a stranded ship. From there, you can see the vast expanse of the ocean and in the distance, you see a whale jumping out of the water and splashing back in. You take a deep breath and feel the warmth of the sun on your skin, and the salty sea breeze in your hair. Then you remember your treasure hunt and explore every bit of the hut until you find a trap door, and underneath a chest filled with gold coins and gleaming jewels.

After you finish your treasure hunt, you return to the pirates, and they tell you that you can keep the riches you found as a reminder of your adventure. You must look hungry because they invite you to join them for a feast. You sit down at the long table and enjoy a delicious meal of seafood and big turkey legs. The pirates tell you all sorts of interesting stories about their adventures on the high seas, like their encounters with sea monsters and sea witches, their search for treasure and the time they saved a whale from hunters. You listen with fascination and ask them hundreds of questions. As you spend time with the pirates, you realize that they are not the scary, villainous pirates you had thought they were. They are kind, generous, and good-hearted and you love the friendship and camaraderie with them. After the feast, the pirates invite you to join them for some music and singing. They pull out their instruments - guitars, drums, and accordions - and start playing pirate songs. You join in, singing and clapping along. The pirates have such fun and energetic personalities that you can't help but get caught up in the joy of the moment.

As the night wears on, you start to feel tired. The pirates notice and invite you to sleep in a hammock strung between two palm trees, so you lie down and snuggle under a soft, cosy blanket. As you go to sleep, you hear the pirates singing and playing their instruments in the distance, now quiet and wistful songs. The sound of their voices and the gentle swaying of the hammock lull you into a deep, peaceful sleep.

As you sink into dreams, imagine the pirate captain, with his long hair, bandana, and eye patch, and think about what his pirate name might be. Imagine the adventures the pirates told you about, the ship they sail on, the treasure they have accumulated on their journey and all the places they have been to. You suddenly realise that the friendship you found here is a much greater treasure than any of the chests of gold and silver they have given you, and with this happy thought, you fall asleep.

Story idea: How did the pirates and the mermaids go from hating each other to helping each other? What common enemy did they fight together?

The Harbour

You walk along the beach to the harbour and soon you see a big sailing ship docked there. The ship is tall and majestic, with billowing white sails and a polished wooden hull, and you a gripped by a longing to join the crew on their journey. There are so many places you could go: the deep, dark jungle (continue below), the snowy arctic (page 68), the endless desert (page 75) or the wild mountains (page 82). The captain invites you on board and asks you: "Where you would like to sail today?"

The Jungle

As soon as you say it, the ship sets off on a journey to the jungle. You feel the ship rock gently as it sets sail, and you hear the sound of the waves lapping against the hull. You see the vast ocean, the endless horizon and the clouds that move swiftly with the wind, and you feel full of wonder and freedom.

Finally, the ship reaches the mouth of a river, and the crew sets anchor and is rowed to the shore in small boats. You disembark and set foot in the jungle, the smell of the earth, the sound of the leaves rustling, and the bright colours of the flowers and fruits are overwhelming. You venture deeper into the dark undergrowth. Colourful birds are singing in the trees, and a river teeming with fish snakes beneath the roof of trees. As you explore, you realise that this is no ordinary jungle. The animals here are magical - a Pegasus grazes on the grass, gryphons soar through the air, and basilisks roam the land.

As you continue to explore the magical jungle, you come across a creature you have never seen before. It has the body of a lion, the wings of a bat and curved horns like an antelope on its head. It is a manticore. The manticore is a fierce and powerful beast, feared by all who encounter it, but as you look into his eyes, you see that they are full of intelligence and kindness. You decide to approach the manticore and offer it a gift - a juicy, ripe fruit. The creature sniffs the fruit and then takes it gently from your hand and there is a connection and understanding between you and the mighty creature.

You spend some time with the manticore, learning more about him and his way of life. You start to understand that this animal is the protector of the jungle, and he has been living here for centuries, keeping it safe from outsiders. The manticore shows you the dangers of the jungle, and how to navigate through it safely. He also guides you to the different magical creatures that live nearby and the hidden treasures that are hidden deep in the jungle.

After exploring the jungle with the powerful beast for a while, you start to feel tired. The manticore notices and offers to take you to a place where you can rest. You gratefully accept and follow the manticore until you come across an abandoned temple hidden deep in the forest. The temple is overgrown with vines and covered in moss, but you can see that it was once a magnificent structure with many stone carvings of animals and plants. The manticore leads you to a room which is small and cosy and has walls adorned with beautiful pictures. You see a comfortable-looking bed in the corner and feel grateful for the manticore's kindness.

You lie down on the bed and close your eyes, feeling the gentle swaying of the vines outside. You hear the sound of the manticore's soft purring next to your bed and your mind is full of peace and contentment.

As you sink into a dream, you try to imagine who built this temple and why. You also think about what other mystical animals live in this jungle and how would it feel to fly on the manticore's back high above the trees. Before you fall asleep you wonder how it would be to live in this place and be a part of this mystical world forever.

Story idea: What would happen if you and the manticore decided to explore the secret tunnels and chambers of this temple? What dangerous traps would you have to escape and what treasure would await you?

The Arctic

The ship soon sets sail to the arctic. On your long way to the colder parts of the world, you meet whales spouting water into the air, and strange seabirds flying overhead. As you sail north, you feel the temperature drop and the days grow shorter. You see the landscape change from green and lush to white and snowy.

You dock the ship and disembark and soon you come across two paths leading in different directions. One path leads to an igloo in the distance (continue below), the other to a snowy hill (page 72). You wonder what adventures await you down each path.

The Igloo

You walk along the path and suddenly a snowstorm rises. The cold wind whips through your hair and the ground is slick and icy under your feet. The snowflakes dance in the air, so dense, it's hard to see anything in front of you. You feel your fingers and toes growing numb and your breath forming frosty clouds in the air. You start to feel hopeless, wondering if you will ever make it through the storm when you spot a round, white structure nestled in the snow. You approach the igloo and knock on the door, and you are surprised when a deep, rumbling voice invites you in.

You enter the igloo and are immediately filled with warmth that spreads to all parts of your body, from the

tip of your nose all the way down to your toes. You see
a cosy, welcoming interior in front of you and the air is
filled with the smell of cooking fish and the sound of
the fire crackling in the hearth. By the fireside, there is
a large, shaggy creature with long white hair and
piercing blue eyes that seems to be roasting some food.
It must be a northern cousin of the famous yeti, who
can normally be found only in the mountains of the
Himalayas. You feel a mix of fear and curiosity as you
look at it. But as you see the yeti's friendly smile, you
decide to go closer.

He introduces itself and invites you to sit by the fire
and even shares a piece of fish with you. You thank the
yeti and take a bite. The fish is delicious - succulent and
flavourful. You feel your body warming up more and
more and your spirits lifting.

As you sit by the fire with the yeti, he begins to tell
you stories from his life. You listen intently, captivated
by his deep, calming voice. Your new friend tells you
about his days in the snowy wilderness, the challenges
he faces, the secrets he has uncovered and the
adventures he has been on. You hear about the time
the yeti got lost in a blizzard and had to find its way
home, about his encounter with a group of polar bears
and how he had to use his cunning and strength to
defend himself, and you hear the story of how he
discovered a secret, hidden cave filled with ancient

artefacts.

While you have been sitting here, listening to adventure stories, the storm has passed and the world outside is transformed. The sun is shining brightly, and the snow glistens in the light. The air is crisp and fresh, and you feel invigorated as you take a deep breath in. The snow crunches under your feet as you walk and the bright sun warms your face, making you squint a little. The sky is a brilliant blue and there is not a cloud in sight. The snow-covered trees and mountains in the distance look like a postcard, and the ground sparkles like diamonds. The sound of the melting snow dripping from the branches and the smell of pine trees and fresh snow fills your nose, with its clean and refreshing aroma. You can't help but feel refreshed by the beauty of the icy landscape. The yeti has followed you and is happy to share more about his culture and way of life. He shows you how he makes his clothes and tools from the materials found in the wilderness, such as furs and bones. He teaches you how to hunt and fish in the snowy terrain and you learn about the different plants that can be used for medicinal purposes and how to make a fire without matches. You also learn how to track different animals and how to read the signs of the weather. You realize that the yeti is not just a creature, but a skilled and knowledgeable being and you wish you could share the yeti's simple way of life in harmony with nature.

Going for a walk through the deep snow is fun, but also hard work and when evening falls, you are glad to return to the warm fire of the igloo. You look around the round room and see a cosy-looking bed made of furs in the corner. The yeti invites you to have a rest there and you lie down on the snuggly bed and close your eyes, feeling the soft, warm furs against your skin. You hear the sound of the fire crackling and the gentle snowfall outside and feel completely safe and protected in here.

As you sleep, you dream of all the adventures the yeti had. You imagine the yeti's escape from the polar bears, what exactly he found in the hidden cave and how the treasure got there. You wonder if the yeti has ever met any other people besides you.

Story idea: What happened when the Yeti discovered he had magical healing properties? What artic animal did he rescue and why did it need rescuing?

Sledging with Elves

You take the climb up the little hill and as you finally reach the top, you are surprised to find a group of elves playing on the other side! You carefully climb down a path to join the little group. The elves are small, mischievous creatures with pointed ears and bright, twinkling eyes. They greet you with warm smiles and invite you to join them and ride a sledge pulled by a team of strong, energetic huskies. You know this is going to be the greatest adventure of your life, so you hop on and take a ride through the snowy landscape.

As you sledge, you see the frozen world fly by: fluffy snow rabbits hiding in snowy burrows and reindeer sheltering under tall, dark fir trees. You can feel the cold wind on your face, but you are snugly wrapped up in warm fur blankets. The elves tell you stories and sing songs as you ride and the world fills with wonder as you listen to their tales and melodies. The elves point out different landmarks and tell you about the history and legends of the arctic. You learn about the different animals that call this place home and the plants that grow here, and you soon feel like you are part of arctic life.

As the night falls around you, you see a faint, glowing light in the distance. You get excited when you realise it is the northern lights curling across the sky. You reach an open area, and you see a beautiful, shimmering display of colours - red, green, blue and purple. They dance and swirl in the sky, creating a mesmerising display. The lights are so bright that they cast a soft glow on everything around you and turn the snowy field into a colourful landscape. As you walk around slowly, you can hear the sound of the snow crunching under your feet and the elves' soft whispers and the huskies' contented sighs. The wind is gentle, and you can hear it rustling through the trees near you. You can't help but feel a sense of peace and joy as you watch the moving aurora borealis in the sky. The colours and movement of the lights have a calming effect, and you feel your mind and body relax. You feel connected to something larger than yourself, and you are grateful for the opportunity to witness this natural wonder.

It is nearly midnight, and you start to feel tired. You see a group of small, cosy huts in the distance and as you get closer you find that it is the elves' village, and you are invited to spend the night in one of the huts. You see a warm, cosy interior with a fire burning in the fireside. You are offered a hot chocolate, with a mountain of whipped cream sprinkled with marshmallows. You drink a sip, and it warms up your whole body from the inside. After you have finished your treat, you lie down on a bed of furs and blankets and close your eyes. You hear the sound of the fire crackling and the elves' soft singing and are completely relaxed and happy.

As you are sinking into dreams, you could think about what adventures you and the elves going to get up to tomorrow. Will they take you to Santa's secret workshop? What presents will you find there? You wonder if you will be able to explain to your family and friends the amazing things you have seen and learned on this trip when you return home to them.

Story idea: How did the elves prevent some hunters from killing some of their arctic animal friends? And what part did the snowy owl play in this?

The Desert

"To the desert!" you call to the captain and soon he lifts the anchor. You see the endless expanse of the sea stretching out before you, and you can smell freedom and adventure.

As the days pass, you see the sea change from a deep blue to a bright, golden colour and soon you spot sandy dunes stretching out before and you are ready to explore.

You take a trek through the desert, and soon feeling the hot sun beating down on you. The sand is soft and shifts under your feet, making it difficult to walk. You feel sweat dripping down your face and your throat is dry and parched. You see the dunes stretching out before you, seeming to go on forever and you start to wonder if you will ever make it out of the desert again. Just then, you see an oasis on the horizon to the left (continue below) and a caravan of traders with camels to the right (page 79). Where are you going to find water and rest?

The Oasis

The way through the desert is difficult, but ahead of you, you see a shimmering pool in the distance, and you know that it is an oasis, a place of rest and refreshment. You quicken your pace and soon climb over the last dune to reach the resting place. You see a

clear, blue pool surrounded by palm trees and lush
vegetation. The oasis is alive with the sound of birds
singing and the rustling of leaves in the breeze. You
reach the edge of the pool and see your reflection in
the water. You see the sweat on your face and the dust
on your clothes, but as soon as you dip your feet in the
water and feel the cool, refreshing liquid wash over
your skin, you are suddenly full of energy again.

You get up and start exploring the oasis. When you
inspect the plants closer, you see some sand lizards
nibbling away at them and you notice that the plants
are growing sweets instead of flowers! You decide to
pluck one of the sweets and take a small bite. It is
absolutely delicious! It has a tangy, sugary flavour and a
smooth texture with a melting centre, and you are
amazed by this new, tasty treat. You decide to try more
of the sweets and find that they all taste fantastic. You
find pink ones, red ones and purple ones, each with its
unique taste and aroma. You follow a small path that
leads you away from the pool and into the heart of the
oasis. You see tall palm trees, exotic vegetation and
more of the colourful sweets. As you walk deeper into
the oasis, you notice a small, shimmering object buried
in the sand. You can't believe your luck when you
realize it's a jewel box. Excitement and curiosity take
over you as you dig the box out of the sand. It's made
of smooth, dark wood and decorated with intricate

carvings. You open the box and see that it's filled with sparkling jewels of all shapes and sizes. There are diamonds, rubies, sapphires and emeralds, all glinting in the sunlight. They are incredibly beautiful, and you feel like a real treasure hunter.

You pick up a ruby and feel its weight in your hand. The crystal is warm from the sun and has a smooth surface. You hold it up to the light and see the way it sparkles, it's like a small sun in your hand. You think about the person who must have buried this box here and wonder what their story was.

You decide to take a couple of the smaller jewels with you as a souvenir of your adventure and put the rest back in the box, covering it back with sand so it can be found by someone else who needs it more than you.

As the night falls, you decide to gather some of the soft leaves that are lying on the ground and make a bed of them to sleep on. You feel the soft, fragrant plants against your skin and a feeling of comfort and contentment washes over you. Above you, you can see the stars so clear and bright like never before with the glowing line of the milky way right above you, and when you suddenly see a shooting star cross the sky, you quickly make a wish.

While falling asleep you could think about what the different plants and sweets looked like and what each one tasted like. You think about the strange, exotic animals living in the oasis. You decide tomorrow, you will go for a swim in the clear water, and you are looking forward to the joy this will bring.

Story idea: Why did a Genie in a lamp have to hide in this oasis? Did he also find the jewel box? And how was he set free from his lamp at the end?

The Caravan

You decide you don't want to be alone in the desert anymore and you walk over to the caravan to ask for help. You see a group of people and animals travelling together, their tents and supplies loaded onto camels and donkeys.

As you come closer, you realise that the camels and the traders are one on the same! These are camel centaurs, their heads and upper body human, with dark hair and mysterious, brown eyes, their back half camels, with soft brown fur. They introduce themselves as camtaurs and invite you to join them on their journey. One of the traders even offers to carry you on his back.

As you ride, you see the sandy dunes stretching out before you, seeming to go on forever, dotted with ancient ruins poking out of the sand, their crumbling walls and pillars telling stories of civilizations long gone, of ancient kings and queens, of battles and conquests, of love and loss.

As you spend time with the camtaurs, you learn that they come from a nomadic tribe that has been travelling the desert for generations. They trade goods and services with the other desert dwellers and are known for their wisdom and knowledge of the desert and its secrets. They tell you about the different animals that live in the desert, from the majestic sand lions to the elusive desert foxes and how they coexist in this harsh environment. The camtaurs also tell you stories about the dangers that lurk here: mighty sandstorms, rushing flash floods and roaming bandits. You are relieved to learn that the Camtaurs are masters in avoiding them and keeping everyone safe.

Soon after dark, you reach a sheltered place and the camtaurs quickly set up a group of tents in a circle, with a comforting fire burning in the middle because the temperature in the desert drops quickly as night falls. You are now part of this warm community as you join them around the fire and share in their delicious stew, and even though you wish you could stay up all night to listen to their stories, your eyelids are starting to droop. The camtaurs notice and invite you to sleep in one of their tents and as you go inside, you see a sleeping area furnished with a comfortable, padded mat and a thick, warm sleeping bag. You see pillows at the head of the mat, and you notice that they are shaped like circles, squares, and triangles, and each one has a different magical symbol embroidered on it. You understand that if you sleep on the symbol of stars, moons, and suns, you will dream of magic and mystery, but if you sleep on the symbols of hearts, diamonds, and spades, you will have a playful dream. Maybe you should sleep on the snakes, dragons, and gryphons to dream of adventure?

You snuggle under your blankets. You close your

eyes and feel the gentle rocking of the tent as you drift off to sleep. As you do so, you try to imagine where the caravan comes from and where is it going. You wonder what treasures they are trading and what would it be like to take part in a camtaur race.

Story idea: Why did the dark magician use his powers to turn a simple market trader into a camtaur? How did the camtaur trick the magician to turn him into a pillar of sandstone?

The Mountains

"I want to visit the mountains," you tell the crew. They lift the anchor, set sails and soon you feel the fresh mountain air blowing through your hair. You disembark the ship and begin your hike through the mountains and the climb is steep and rocky, but you're determined to reach the summit. You feel the burn in your legs as you climb higher and higher, but you know the view from the top will be worth it.

As you are halfway up the mountain, the path splits into three. Straight ahead, you can see a team getting a hot air balloon ready for departure to take you to the top (continue below). To your left, you see a path that seems to lead to a cave with mysterious smoke coming out of it (page 86). The right leads down to a secluded valley, and you think you can see a unicorn horn sticking out from behind a bush (page 89). Which way are you going?

The Hot Air Balloon

You approach the colourful hot air balloon with a feeling of wonder and excitement. The fabric of the balloon is gently billowing in the breeze, and you can't help but smile at the thought of embarking on this magical journey. You climb into the basket, eager to take off and soar into the sky. As you start to lift off the ground, you feel weightless and free, leaving all your worries and cares behind. You see the world below you gradually sink away as you rise higher and higher into the sky.

The view from above is simply breathtaking. You see the blue sky stretching out above you, dotted with fluffy white clouds, and the green treetops below. The world looks different from up here, peaceful and quiet. As you continue to rise, a majestic mountain peak comes into view. You feel a sense of accomplishment as you soar over the peak, taking in the beauty of the snowy rocks and the vast expanse of the world below.

Just when you fly over the mountain peak, you suddenly see tiny figures below. They are dwarves, dressed in bright red jackets and brown boots, hard at work in the mountains. They are using hammers and chisels to carve tunnels into the rock. The tunnels they are creating are like roads, allowing the dwarves to travel deep into the mountain where they can find precious gems and minerals. Even from up here, you can see they are working together in harmony, each performing a specific task. Some dwarves are using pickaxes to break large rocks into smaller pieces, while others are loading the pieces into carts. The carts are then pulled by strong mules, who are specially trained to navigate the steep mountain paths. The dwarves take turns resting and enjoying the beautiful mountain scenery. They sing songs, play musical instruments, and even have picnics under the shade of nearby trees.

Your heart fills with happiness as you watch the dwarves work, play, and live in harmony with nature. You realise that despite their small size, they have a big impact on the world and the people around them.

Soon the dwarves and the mountain peak glide out of view, and you start to feel tiredness wash over you. You know it's time to find a place to rest, so you look down and see a serene lake below. You guide the balloon towards the lake, eager to touch down on its grassy shore. Approaching the shore, you see a tree house nestled in the branches of a tall oak. The tree house is made of sturdy wooden planks, and its roof is covered in leaves and moss. The windows are round and inviting, glowing warm and golden from a fireside inside. The entrance to the cabin is a wooden ladder that leads up to a platform that serves as the front porch. From here, you can see the lake and the surrounding forest, and the sounds of birds singing, and leaves rustling fills the air. Inside you find a cosy bunk bed and shelves full of books and as you lie down on the bed, you feel the soft sheets against your skin. You close your eyes and listen to the sound of the breeze rustling the leaves outside. You feel a sense of peace and contentment wash over you as you drift off into a deep and restful sleep.

As you sleep, your mind drifts to all the adventures that await you in this world. Imagine flying over a bustling dwarf town, what would you see down there? Where would you go if you could travel anywhere you liked? What other creatures did you see when you flew over the mountains? Allow your mind to wander and let the peaceful feeling of the cabin and the sound of the wind carry you into a deep and restful sleep.

Story idea: What happened when three adventurers decided to fly around the world in their balloon? In which country did they crash land and who did they meet there?

The Dragon

As you climb up the path, the small cave opening grows larger and clearer, and you can see gentle rings of smoke coming out of it. You approach the entrance with a sense of curiosity and awe, knowing that this will be an adventure unlike any other. You take a deep breath and step inside the cave, letting your eyes adjust to the dim light that filters in through the entrance.

As you look around, you see a magnificent dragon curled up on a bed of gold and jewels. The dragon is covered in shimmering scales, and its wings are folded neatly against its body. The creature stirs and opens its eyes, and calm washes over you as you look into its wise and graceful gaze.

The dragon is a magnificent creature, with shimmering, emerald green scales that reflect the dim light filtering in through the cave entrance. Its wings are huge and with swirling patterns, and a soft golden glow along the edges. He has deep-set eyes that sparkle like diamonds, and its eyes are a warm, golden-brown colour. His horns are long and curving with shimmering spirals going up, giving it a regal appearance, and his tail is long and flexible, curled around his body.

You step closer to the dragon, drawn in by its aura of power and wisdom. He beckons you with a gentle nod of his head, and you reach out to touch his scales.

As your fingers brush against the dragon's skin, you feel a surge of strength and courage flow through you, and you know that this being is a powerful ally. The dragon speaks to you in a language that you do not understand, yet you can feel the meaning behind its words, and he shares his wisdom and knowledge with you, and your mind is expanding with understanding.

You look around and realise that the cave is a wondrous and magical place. The walls and ceiling are made of rough, natural stone, but there is something else that sets this cave apart from any other. There are veins of solid gold running through the rock, reflecting the dim light and casting a warm, golden glow throughout the space. The gold glimmers and sparkles and the effect is mesmerising. The air is cool and still, and there's a gentle trickle of water coming from a small stream that runs through the cave. The sound of the stream is calming and soothing, and you feel at peace as you explore this magical place. The walls are dotted with gems of all colours, and there's a bed of gold and jewels in the centre of the cave where the dragon rests. The treasure trove is awe-inspiring, but it's the dragon's presence that truly makes this cave special. As you wander deeper into the cave, you find a secluded corner that is away from the dragon's hoard of treasures. The walls and floor are smooth and covered in a soft glow from some sort of moss or lichen growing there and you feel the presence of a peaceful energy in this place. You decide to make this your resting spot for the night, and you lay down on the mossy bed and close your eyes.

The gentle sound of the stream inside the cave and the dragon's soft breathing combine to create a soothing ambience. You feel safe and protected, knowing that the dragon will watch over you as you sleep in his cave. You drift off to sleep, you think back to how beautiful the dragon looked and you marvel at the colour of its scales. You wonder what kind of treasures can be found in this cave. Are there any magical and precious items here that are not just coins and crowns?

Story idea: The dragon did not steal the treasure – it was a reward for rescuing a powerful king – how did he help him and why did the king need the dragon to save him?

The Unicorns

You keep climbing a bit further up the steep path, and as you reach the top of the ridge, you are awestruck by the beauty of the valley that unfolds before you. The tall green grass shimmers and dances in the gentle breeze, while streams of crystal-clear water run between banks dotted with flowers of every shade. The colours are so vibrant, so rich, that it seems as if a master painter had carefully crafted each petal and blade of grass.

As you move closer, you spot a group of unicorns in the distance, gracefully grazing and basking in the warm sun. They look up as you approach, and instead of running away, they come to greet you. Their fur is glistening gold, and their eyes are the purest blue you have ever seen. They nuzzle your hand, and you feel their magic energy flow through you. It's as if they've been waiting for you, and all your worries disappear as you bask in their presence.

The unicorns invite you to play a game of tag, and you join in, amazed by their speed and grace. They dart and weave through the valley with ease, their manes and tails flowing behind them. It feels as if they are barely touching the ground as they run, and their playfulness is infectious. You can't help but smile and laugh as you run and dodge alongside them, and the sense of carefree joy you feel is like nothing you've ever experienced before.

The unicorns are full of surprises. They have unique abilities to control and harness nature's elements, and they often use their powers to make their games even more fun. They use their magic to change the direction of the wind to blow into their pursuers face, or they create trails of flowers that lead them to the next player, and they are made up of tiny flowers, sparkling leaves, and glittering gems that glimmer and twinkle in the light. When the unicorns play hide and seek, they use their powers to make themselves invisible or to create illusions to confuse their opponents. They are also known to create rainbows in the sky to celebrate the end of the game, or to create gardens of the most fragrant and beautiful flowers that bloom just for a moment, before disappearing into the air. As you observe their playful powers, you feel amazed by their creativity, and the joy and happiness radiating from them. The unicorns truly make the valley a magical and enchanted place, and you are lucky to be a part of it.

As the sun begins to dip below the horizon, the unicorns invite you to rest among the wildflowers for the night. The petals of the flowers are soft and velvety to the touch, and they give off a sweet, floral scent. The animals gather around you as you lie down in the soft grass, and you feel their gentle, healing magic encircling you. Your body and mind relax completely, and you fall into a deep, restful sleep.

As you are waiting for your dreams, you imagine the unicorns in more detail. What does each one look like? Do they have different colours, patterns, and markings? Do some of them have wings? And what other games do they like to play? What about the flowers in this valley? Are they different from any flowers you have seen before? What shapes and colours do they have?

Story idea: The unicorns used to live in a forest a long way from here. Why did they have to leave that forest and what adventures did they meet on their way? How did they find this secret valley in the mountains?

Portal to Distant Times

You step through the shimmering green portal and find yourself in a stunning room that's entirely bathed in a rich, green glow. As you look around, you see that there are four doors, one on each wall. The first door, made from rugged stone, has a sign hanging above it that reads "Jurassic Period" (continue below). The second door, constructed from fine, white sandstone, bears the inscription "Ancient Egypt" (page 99). The third door, a heavy wooden one, is labelled "Middle Ages"(page 106). And finally, in front of you, stands a gleaming metal door, which has the word "Future" etched upon it (page 113). You feel a thrill of excitement at the possibilities that await you. Which door are you stepping through today?

Jurassic Period

You step through the door made from rocks and immediately find yourself in a dense jungle where the air is filled with all kinds of noises. To the left, you can hear the gentle grunts of a group of large dinosaurs (page 96) and to the right, you can hear the rumbling of a volcano (continue below), which way are you taking?

The Volcano

You make your way through the dense jungle, admiring the beauty of the plants and trees as you go. You climb over tree roots and duck under long hanging branches, taking in the sights and sounds of the forest. Suddenly, you spot a stunning creature in the distance. It's a pterodactyl [teh·ruh·dak·tl] with huge wings and a long tail, and it's sitting on a branch, waiting for you.

You approach the pterodactyl, and it lets out a soft chirp, inviting you to climb on its back. It is a beautiful creature, with shimmering, iridescent green feathers covering its body, and its eyes are a dark, shining black. You hesitate for a moment, but then you remember why you're here, and you climb on the animal's back.

The pterodactyl takes off, and you feel the wind rushing past your face and the sun on your skin. You fly over a lush, green forest, where you can see different species of dinosaurs roaming around. You see a herd of triceratops, a family of velociraptors, and a group of stegosauruses, all going about their daily lives.

As you continue your journey, you see a volcano in the distance. It's tall and smoking, and you can feel the heat even from this far away. The pterodactyl flies closer and closer, giving you a chance to take a good look at the volcano. You see different shades of red, orange, and yellow in the lava, and you can hear the rumbling sound it makes as it flows down the sides.

You see the different shapes the lava makes as it flows and you feel the heat on your skin and smell the sulphur, but you still feel safe and secure, as the pterodactyl is a skilled flier and knows how to avoid the dangerous parts.

You marvel at the sheer size and power of this natural wonder. From above, the volcano looks even more massive, with its steep slopes and vast crater. You see the ash clouds rising high into the sky, and the plumes of smoke wafting in the wind. The landscape around the volcano is desolate, with little vegetation and blackened earth, a testament to the power of the eruption. But as you fly closer, you see small signs of life returning, with seedlings of green plants emerging from the ash and tiny creatures scurrying around. It is a breathtaking sight, to see the delicate balance between destruction and renewal, and you feel humbled to be able to witness it from the back of the magnificent pterodactyl.

After flying around the volcano, the pterodactyl starts to head back to its home. You can see in the distance a large cliff, and as you get closer, you realize that it's the creature's nest. It lands gently on the edge of the cliff, and you get off. You see that the nest is made out of soft fern leaves and mosses, and it's big enough for you to lie down in. You rest your head on the leaves, feeling tired from the flight and the

94

excitement of the volcano, and you close your eyes, listening to the rhythm of the pterodactyl's breathing beside you. You know it will watch over you while you rest.

As you drift off to sleep, you are thinking about the dinosaurs you saw in the jungle below and what the future holds for this magical world. You wonder what else you could see from the sky if you took another flight with the pterodactyl and what it would be like to be able to fly yourself.

Story idea: What happened when the pterodactyl tried to find a mate? Why did he have to trick a T-Rex to win her over and how did he do it?

The Dinosaurs

You approach the sounds and soon come across a group of friendly stegosauruses. They are big and grey, with long necks and spikes on their back. As you approach, they notice you and come over to greet you with gentle nudges from their snouts. They move gracefully around you, and you can tell that these creatures are curious and friendly. They seem to want to show you something, and so you follow them deeper into the forest.

You walk among the trees, surrounded by the sounds of creatures calling and leaves swaying overhead. You see other dinosaurs in the distance, but the stegosauruses seem unfazed, confident in their strength and spiky armour, even when a T-Rex walks by in the distance.

As you are following this family of stegosauruses, you observe their interactions with each other. They communicate through gentle nudges and low, rumbling sounds. The mother stegosaurus is fiercely protective of her young and they follow her lead. The father stegosaurus takes on a more nurturing role, and he is often seen helping the little ones reach leaves that are out of their reach. You are captivated by the love and care that they have for each other and the way they work together to ensure their group's safety and well-being. The family dynamic is strong, and you are so happy that you can be part of it today.

They lead you through the jungle, to a big cave that shines with a beautiful crystal light. As you get closer, you see the cave walls are covered in an array of crystals in different colours and shapes and the light reflects on them, creating a rainbow effect. The stegosauruses invite you to explore the cave, showing you the different crystals, each with its unique power and energy.

After this long walk through the jungle, you feel you need a nap. In a secluded alcove, surrounded by crystals, you find a peaceful and calming atmosphere. The crystals shine a soft light, and you lie down on soft moss and ferns. The stegosauruses stay with you, keeping watch and ensuring you are safe and comfortable. You close your eyes and allow yourself to drift off to sleep.

As you fall asleep, you ponder what it must be like to be a young stegosaurus and to play in the jungle. You also think back to the colours and shapes of crystals you saw in the cave. Which crystal would you like to have in your room? What power and energy would they possess?

Story idea: What adventures happened to the stegosaurus family when they had to leave their forest to escape the volcanic eruption? How did each family member contribute to their escape?

Ancient Egypt

You step through the stone door and find yourself in ancient Egypt, standing in front of the River Nile. You see a boat with a sail, decorated with hieroglyphs and ready to take you to the pyramids (continue below). You also see an ancient temple with a mysterious statue (page 103). Are you going to take the boat or explore the temple?

The Boat

As you step onto the boat, the warm sun envelopes your skin and the soft breeze caresses your hair. The boatman greets you with a smile and explains that the pyramids are a place of great significance, steeped in history and surrounded by mystery. You take a seat in the bow and gaze upon the Nile, with its lush green palm trees along the riverbank and the vibrant birds soaring overhead. The steady swaying of the boat creates a tranquil and peaceful atmosphere.

As you sail closer to the pyramids, their enormity becomes more and more impressive. The Great Pyramid of Giza, the Pyramid of Khafre, and the Sphinx standing guard in front of them, all make for a truly awe-inspiring sight. You can see people of all ages visiting the pyramids, entering and exiting as if they are portals to another world.

When you reach the monuments, you are struck by

their grandeur and architectural power. There are workmen inside carefully decorating the tombs with precision and skill and you are invited to step inside and witness their handiwork. In the tunnels, your eyes are drawn to the elaborate decorations that adorn the walls and ceilings. The workmen, with their brushes and chisels, are busy at work, bringing the ancient scenes to life. The walls are covered in intricate paintings depicting the pharaohs and the gods they worship. You can see paintings of the pharaoh hunting lions, and offerings being made to the gods in a grand temple. The gold and vibrant colours used in the pictures glisten in the dim light, adding to the grandeur of the place.

The workmen are also in the process of placing various treasures in the tombs. The air is filled with the sound of clinking as they carry in amphoras, large pottery jars used to store wine, oil, or grains, which and are intricately decorated with scenes of the pharaohs and their accomplishments. The workmen place the amphoras in specific spots within the tombs, taking care to ensure that they are properly aligned.

Alongside the containers, the workmen are also bringing in golden statues, and you can see the intricate details and the craftsmanship that went into creating these masterpieces. The golden light reflecting off them illuminates the room and you stand there in awe, taking in the beauty and wonder of this ancient place.

As you say goodbye to the workmen and leave the tomb, one of them kindly offers for you to spend the night with his family in their cottage located near the pyramids. You follow him to his humble abode, made of mudbrick with a thatched roof, and his wife and children welcome you in. You are greeted by the warm aroma of bread baking in the oven and the flickering of a small fire in the fireplace. They kindly share their meal of flatbread, lentils and fresh fruit with you and the workman's children look at you with curiosity while you eat. After the meal, you listen to the father tell his children a bedtime story, and even though you don't understand his language, his calming tones soon make you want to fall asleep, just like his children. You lie down on one of the comfy beds and you can hear the soothing sound of the River Nile splashing against its banks and the melodious chorus of cicadas singing in the background.

As you drift off to sleep, you reflect on the day's events. The vibrant life along the Nile, the people and animals you encountered on the boat ride, the intricate scenes painted inside the pyramid, and the untold treasures stored within its walls. It has been a day filled with adventure and discovery, and you can't wait to see what tomorrow will bring.

Story idea: What happens when a group of

workmen's children stumble upon a secret chamber hidden deep within the pyramid and must navigate a series of challenges and puzzles to uncover its long-forgotten secrets?

The Temple

As you walk along the riverbank, you approach a magnificent temple that catches your attention. In front of the temple, you see a young pharaoh, dressed in regal attire with a golden crown upon his head and a sturdy staff in hand. The pharaoh notices you and comes over to greet you, introducing himself as King Tutankhamun. He is eager to show you around the temple, dedicated to the gods who protected and blessed the pharaohs and the people of ancient Egypt.

You follow the young pharaoh into the temple, and you are immediately awed by the towering pillars, grand statues, and mysterious hieroglyphs that adorn the walls. The intricate carvings of the gods, such as Ra, the god of the sun, and Osiris, the god of the afterlife, can be seen everywhere. Tutankhamun shares with you the history and culture of ancient Egypt and explains the gods' importance in everyday life.

As the day draws to a close and it is time to say goodbye, Tutankhamun reveals one final surprise. He takes you to a secret chamber within the temple, and as you enter the room, you see a figure standing in front of you. The figure is tall and slender, with the head of an ibis, a sacred bird of ancient Egypt. The ibis has a long beak like a heron, and the figure is holding a writing palette and a reed pen, symbols of wisdom, writing, and knowledge. The figure is dressed in a long white robe, adorned with gold and precious stones, and has a peaceful and wise expression on his face. The figure is Thoth, the god of wisdom, and he greets you with a kind smile, making you feel at ease. Thoth speaks to you in a gentle voice, and shares a message of wisdom with you, reminding you that the key to understanding the world is through learning and growth. Thoth also gives you a small token, a feather, as a reminder of your meeting with him.

You are filled with awe and wonder at having met a god, and you can feel the wisdom and power of Thoth radiating around you. You thank Tutankhamun and Thoth for the incredible day, and you take the feather as a cherished reminder of your special visit.

Darkness has started to fall, and Tutankhamun offers to show you where you can sleep for the night, so he takes you to the grand palace. He realises that you must be hungry after your exciting day in Egypt and shares an amazing meal with you, consisting of traditional foods such as flatbread, beans, and pomegranate salad. The food is delicious and satisfying, and you enjoy your time with the pharaoh. After your meal, you walk through the palace to your bed chamber, and you are greeted by a beautiful and comfortable space. The room has a large bed and a balcony that overlooks the serene palace gardens, and you can see the light of the stars and moon shining through the window.

As you lie in bed, you allow your imagination to wander, thinking about the rooms in the temple, the wall paintings and the beauty of the palace gardens. You even imagine what it would be like to be pharaoh for a day, experiencing all the power and grandeur of ancient Egypt.

Story idea: What happens when a young prince, who is visiting the palace for the first time, gets lost in its maze-like corridors and must rely on his wit and the help of the palace's inhabitants to find his way back to his chambers before his father, the pharaoh, returns from the hunt?

The Middle Ages

You step through the strong, wooden door and find yourself standing in front of a grand castle. The walls are surrounded by a moat with a drawbridge and can see the flag of the kingdom flying on top of the tallest tower.

You walk across the drawbridge and enter the castle into a big courtyard, where you can see knights training and people going about their daily business. Do you continue to explore the castle (continue below), or do you stay with the knights (page 110)?

The Castle

As you continue to take a walk across the yard, you are in awe of the many activities taking place. The stable is bustling with activity as grooms care for the horses and brush their coats until they gleam. Meanwhile, the blacksmith is hammering away at his forge, his muscles flexing as he crafts weapons and tools. The sweet scent of baking bread wafts from the kitchen, and the sound of minstrels playing music adds to the festive atmosphere.

Making your way inside the castle, you come across the great hall, where a long table is set with a feast fit for royalty. Plates of roasted meats, bowls of fresh vegetables, and loaves of steaming bread are artfully arranged on the table, tempting you with their delicious aromas. You can hear your stomach grumbling as you take in the sight.

The lords and ladies of the castle are seated at the table, dressed in their finest attire. The men wear tunics, while the women are adorned in veils and long dresses made of the finest silk. They are chatting and laughing, clearly enjoying each other's company. You spot the lord of the castle, seated at the head of the table, and the lady of the castle by his side. Both wear ornate crowns, and they beckon you to join them at the feast.

As the lords and ladies dine, the musicians play in the background, their instruments creating a harmonious melody. The lute and the flute blend together as the minstrels sing songs and tell stories and prompt laughter and applause from the assembled guests. However, the entertainment does not stop there. Suddenly, a jester enters the room, juggling fruits and vegetables then he drops them all on his head and his silly face makes you laugh out loud. Next, a magician comes in, and the crowd's attention turns to him. He starts performing illusions, pulling coins out of the air and making doves appear out of nowhere. The lords and ladies are amazed, and they are clapping and cheering. The magician's finale is the most incredible one yet, as he makes a horse disappear and then reappear in an instant at the other end of the hall. The crowd erupts in applause, and you can feel the excitement in the air.

As you take part in the feast, you feel yourself getting lost in the moment, surrounded by a sense of belonging, community, and happiness. The food is delicious, and the company is even better. When the feast finally comes to an end, the lord and lady of the castle invite you to stay the night in one of the castle's bedrooms.

You follow them to one of the towers, where you ascend a spiralling staircase until you reach a cosy, comfortable bedroom. Tapestries adorn the walls, and a massive four-poster bed sits in the centre of the room, its thick quilt and plumped pillows inviting you to rest. Climbing into the bed, you close your eyes and let yourself drift off to sleep, lulled by the sweet song of a nightingale outside.

As you slumber, your mind begins to wander, imagining the other rooms within the castle. You wonder what they look like and who is working in the kitchens and gardens. You imagine the lush greenery of the garden, wondering what plants and flowers are growing there. You fall asleep, eager to explore more of the castle and its secrets in the morning.

Story idea: The lady of this castle is secretly a good witch who can do healing magic. What happens when her husband finds out and how does she rescue the kingdom?

The Knights

You decide to meet the knights. You see one in very shining armour, holding a long sword and a heavy shield. He notices you and he comes over to greet you. The knight introduces himself as Sir Reginald of the Radiant Shield and he tells you that he is looking for an apprentice for the day. He explains that he will teach you how to be a knight and you eagerly accept his offer.

Sir Reginald takes you around the castle's courtyard, where you see many other knights in training. You begin your day as an apprentice knight with Sir Reginald by learning the basics of horsemanship. He takes you to the stables where you meet a beautiful chestnut horse, who will be your companion for the day. Sir Reginald teaches you how to groom and care for your trusty steed, and you learn about the different equipment you will need for riding. He then shows you how to mount and dismount the horse, and how to control its speed and direction. You practice walking, trotting and cantering, and Sir Reginald corrects your posture and technique along the way.

Next, you move on to learning the skills of sword fighting. You start with simple exercises, such as thrusts and parries, and gradually work your way up to more advanced moves. Sir Reginald emphasises the importance of footwork, balance, and coordination in sword fighting, and he helps you improve your stance and grip on the sword. You learn about the importance of being strong, brave, and respectful as a knight and about the code of chivalry, a set of principles such as loyalty, courtesy, and protection of the vulnerable.

You spend the rest of the day practising these skills, both on horseback and on foot. You learn how to charge with a lance, how to defend against multiple opponents, and how to use your horse in battle. You also take part in mock combat, where you have the chance to put your newfound skills to the test. As the training comes to an end, you feel confident and ready to face any challenge as a knight. Sir Reginald gives you a small token, a medallion, as a reminder of your day as an apprentice. He tells you that you can always come back to the castle and visit him again.

He then takes you on a tour of the castle, showing you the different rooms, such as the great hall, the chapel, and the kitchen. He introduces you to the lords and ladies of the castle, and he tells you about their roles and responsibilities. In the end, he gives you a comfortable room with a big four-poster bed, where you quickly fall asleep, exhausted from swinging your sword.

As you are getting more and more sleepy, you remember the day with all the different activities you and the other knights did. You think back to all rooms the knight showed you in the castle and you remember how you meet some of the other young squires the same age as you and how fun it was to practise together.

Story idea: What happens when a group of brave young squires, who are training to become knights, discover a secret passageway in the castle that leads to a hidden treasure?

The Future

As you walk through the door into the future, you arrive at a kind of transport hub and are greeted by a woman in a strange and shiny metallic outfit, and she tells you that different parts of the earth have developed in very different ways. You can either visit a technologically advanced robot town called Techtopia (continue below) or you can travel to Ecopolis, a city where people now live in harmony with nature (page 118). Which one would you like to visit?

Techtopia

As you prepare to embark on your journey to the futuristic city of Techtopia, you can't wait for the thrill of exploring a place where robots live and work together in unity. You take the rocket train, and soon you glide along between tall, gleaming buildings of metal and glass. You step out of the carriage and start wandering the streets, among the constant whirring and clanking of gears and motors, as robots of all shapes and sizes bustle about their daily business. From two-legged robots walking on the road to wheeled robots trundling past, and even flying robots soaring above, the city is a never-ending display of technology in motion.

You're immediately struck by the air of innovation and progress in every corner of Techtopia. Robot workshops are filled with mechanical men repairing and building new machines, while research labs teem with robots conducting experiments and working on cutting-edge projects. And in the factories, automated machines are manufacturing products that are both useful and beautiful. Everywhere you look, you can see robots working together to create and build, and you feel a sense of awe at the sheer creativity and efficiency of it all.

As you explore, you come across a computer lab and are greeted by an android who warmly invites you to step inside and create your very own virtual reality computer game. The robot explains that the possibilities are endless, and you can create a game about anything you can imagine. With the robots' help, you can choose the graphics, program the characters, and design the levels. And you don't just sit at a screen, but you can step right into the virtual world! And before you know it, you're fully immersed in your game, using your hands to conjure up objects and characters that appear before you. You feel like a master creator as you design obstacles, write the story, choose the music and sound effects, and fine-tune every aspect of your game.

As the day draws to a close, the robots test your game and are thoroughly impressed. They tell you how much they love it, and you feel a rush of pride and happiness. You realise that you've created something truly special and that this experience will stay with you forever.

You are not quite tired yet, so you decide to explore a bit more. You walk down wide, clean streets lined with bustling shops, cafes, and interactive holographic billboards. You visit the central park, where robots and visitors alike gather to relax, play, and enjoy the natural beauty of the surrounding gardens and fountains. You walk down a quiet side street and come across a large building with a sign that reads "Robot Museum." You decide to visit and enter the museum, where you learn about the history of robots and their evolution over the years. There are interactive displays and exhibits that showcase the different types of robots and their uses in various industries and fields. You are fascinated by the information and amazed at how far technology has come. The museum even has a section dedicated to the history of Techtopia, with exhibits explaining the various innovations and breakthroughs that have been made in the town over the years. You leave the museum feeling informed and inspired.

It is quite late now, and you decide to stay in a robo-hotel, a sleek and modern building, with rooms specifically designed for visitors like you. Your room is equipped with a comfortable hover bed that floats just above the ground, glowing gently in the dark. With its control panel, you can adjust the height, position, temperature, and lighting, and even enjoy a built-in massage function to help you relax and fall asleep more easily. The hover bed also features a transparent canopy that can be raised or lowered, perfect for stargazing or taking in the stunning views of the city's lights and screens. You feel weightless and comfortable as you sink into the bed, and you're grateful for the opportunity to experience the advanced technology of Techtopia.

As you drift off to sleep, let your mind wander back to all the sights and sounds of the city. Think about the awe-inspiring buildings, the robots working tirelessly in their workshops, and the endless possibilities of your computer game. And remember that, in Techtopia, anything is possible.

Story idea: What happens when a creative little robot who doesn't like ordinary robot life decides to go on a secret adventure to explore the forbidden zones of Techtopia and discovers the city's mysterious past?

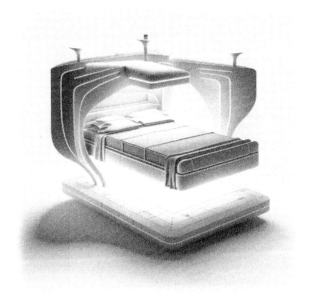

Ecopolis

A fast shuttle takes you on a journey to a place called Ecopolis, where humans and nature live in perfect harmony. As you step off the train, your eyes are met with towering structures made of thriving green plants and trees. The air is filled with the flutter of brightly coloured butterflies and the chirping of birds, while streams flow freely through the streets, ending in crystal-clear ponds.

As you explore the city, you witness the residents walking and biking, all dressed in vibrant hues, with happy and healthy expressions. They are engaged in conversation, caring for their plants and animals, and working together to keep their city clean and green.

You stumble upon a lush park, where a big playground and a tranquil lake invite you in. You can see children playing and laughing on the swings and you join them for some of their games. The playground in Ecopolis is unlike any other you have ever seen. It is surrounded by lush, green vegetation and is dotted with towering trees that provide shade and a natural environment for play. There are swings and slides made from smooth wood and ropes woven from strong, natural fibres. The ground is soft and spongy, covered in a thick layer of grass and flowers, and is perfect for running and jumping on.

There is a big mud puddle, which is the best part of

the playground. Children run to it with excitement, eager to play in the cool, squishy mud. They use their hands and feet to create mud sculptures and build towers, their faces alight with delight as they explore their creativity. Parents watch from nearby, smiling as they see their children experiencing the joy of playing in nature. You can't resist the temptation and take your shoes off to step into the puddle. Walking barefoot through the mud feels soft and squashy between your toes, as the cool and damp earth hugs the soles of your feet. Your sink in with each step, creating a satisfying sensation as the mud gently massages your feet. With every movement, your toes grip the soft soil, and you can feel the texture of the ground beneath you. You can hear the sound of the mud squishing and splashing as you walk. It's an earthy and grounding experience, connecting you to the natural environment around you.

You join a group of children playing here and they ask you lots of questions and are curious about where you are from and why you are visiting their city. You tell them about your journey and how you are fascinated by their city's harmony between people and nature. Together you go to the pond and watch the exotic fish with their long swaying tails circling in the water and wash your feet and dry them in the sun until you can put your shoes back on. Then the group of children takes you to a farmer's market, where one of their mums is selling fruits, vegetables and bread and she gives each of you a strange, but delicious-looking fruit. When you bite into it, it is refreshing and sweet, the best fruit you have ever tasted. Everywhere on the market square people are sitting and eating together, and you can feel the sense of community and friendship among them.

As night falls, one of the children invites you to stay in their living eco-house, built entirely from natural materials like plants, earth, and wood. The walls are made of mud and straw, and the roof is covered in grass. Your host shows you to a guest room with a bed unlike any other you've ever seen. It's made completely from plants and smells of fresh herbs, with leaves and flowers forming a roof like a four-poster bed. You feel grateful for the chance to rest in this special bed as the soft sound of gentle rain lulls you to sleep.

As you drift off, your mind begins to wander, imagining the other buildings in the town and what a school in Ecopolis might look like. You wonder what kind of lessons you would learn in their school and what the adults in the city do for a living. You try to imagine what it would be like to live in harmony with nature every day and how you could look after your patch of greenery and the animals that live in it.

Story idea: What happens when the group of children from Ecopolis discover a secret plot by a company to destroy a nearby forest and build a factory? How do they work together to stop it and save their beloved wood and build a special playground in it?

Acknowledgement

I would like to say thank you to my family, especially my two children who have inspired me to write this book and who have experienced all the dreams with me.

I would also express my gratitude to OpenAI's language model, GPT-3 and the team behind it, for its contribution to this book. This model helped me with the organisation of thoughts, the flow of the text, and the development of the magical places.

I would also like to thank the AI image generator "Midjourney" and the people who created it, for the beautiful illustrations in this book, which I hope will inspire children's happy dreams.

I hope you and your children have enjoyed this book together.

I would be thrilled if you would share any pictures or stories that your children have created after listening to one of the stories. If you're interested in doing so, please reach out to me through my website https://chooseyourowndream.wordpress.com. Please let me know if you're comfortable with me publishing your child's work on this website, along with their first name and age.

The Mindmap

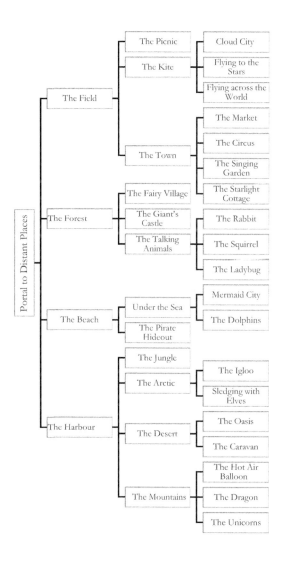

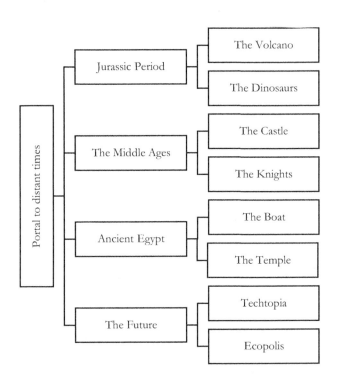